*To Harriet Fisher — W.E.*

Inspired by Kenyon Cox's *Mixed Beasts* published in 1904

Illustrations © 2005 Wallace Edwards

Kids Can Press acknowledges the financial support of the Government of Ontario, through the Ontario Media Development Corporation's Ontario Book Initiative; the Ontario Arts Council; the Canada Council for the Arts; and the Government of Canada, through the BPIDP, for our publishing activity.

Published in Canada by
Kids Can Press Ltd.
29 Birch Avenue
Toronto, ON  M4V 1E2

Published in the U.S. by
Kids Can Press Ltd.
2250 Military Road
Tonawanda, NY  14150

www.kidscanpress.com

The artwork in this book was rendered in watercolor, colored pencil and gouache.
The text is set in Celeste and Edwardian Script.

Edited by Tara Walker
Designed by Karen Powers
Printed and bound in China

This book is smyth sewn casebound.

CM 05  0 9 8 7 6 5 4 3 2 1

**Library and Archives Canada Cataloguing in Publication**

Cox, Kenyon, 1856–1919.
Mixed beasts / written by Kenyon Cox ; illustrated by Wallace Edwards.

ISBN 1-55337-796-6

1. Animals — Juvenile poetry. I. Edwards, Wallace II. Title.

PZ8.3.C83Mi 2005  j811'.52  C2004-906566-1

Kids Can Press is a **Corus**™ Entertainment company

# *Mixed* BEASTS

## Or, a Miscellany of Rare and Fantastic Creatures

COMPILED BY

PROFESSOR JULIUS DUCKWORTH O'HARE, ESQ.

*Illustrations by*

WALLACE EDWARDS

*Verses by*

KENYON COX

KIDS CAN PRESS

## The Rhinocerostrich

He surely is not built for speed;
I don't, myself, think him a beauty;
His strongest traits are wrath and greed;
Yet, I suppose, he does his duty.

## The Octopussycat

I love Octopussy, his arms are so long;
There's nothing in nature so sweet as his song.
'Tis true I'd not touch him — no, not for a farm!
If I keep at a distance he'll do me no harm.

## The Hornbillygoat

Though he's handsome and bold
And protected from cold,
This creature is far from jolly.
It's the curl of his toes
And the hump on his nose
That cause his melancholy.

## The Bumblebeaver

A cheerful and industrious beast,
He's always humming as he goes
To make mud-houses with his tail
Or gather honey with his nose.

Although he flits from flower to flower
He's not at all a gay deceiver.
We might take lessons by the hour
From busy, buzzy Bumblebeaver.

# The Kangarooster

His tail is remarkably long
And his legs are remarkably strong;
But the strength and the length
of his legs and his tail
Are as naught to the strength of his song.

He picks up his food with his bill;
He bounds over valley and hill;
But the height of his bounds
can't compare with the sounds
He lets out when he crows with a will.

## The Peanuthatch

This funny bird lives upside down
And makes his nest in a paper bag.
He never, never wags his tail,
Because he hasn't one to wag.

## The Creampuffin

He migrates in a baker's cart;
He has no wings or feet;
He's round and fat and foolish,
But he's very good — to eat.

## The Parrotter

The Parrotter can potter
About in the water,
Where his coat of green
Makes him quite unseen.

His natural voice is but seldom heard,
But, properly trained, he can talk "like a bird";
And thus he expresses his natural wish:
"Pretty Poll! Pretty Poll! Polly want fish!"

## The Hippopotamustang

O children, note his cheerful smile —
You never hear this beast complain.
He gallops gayly for a mile
With swishing tail and flying mane,
Then stows away a ton of hay
And so begins to smile again.

## The Camelephant

This is the ship of the jungle,
Whose form is much of a bungle.
He never is happy except when in bed,
For it takes all his strength to hold up his head.

# The Flamingocart

This kindly bird does what he can,
Regardless of the jeers of gabies,
To show himself the friend of man —
At any rate the friend of babies.

## The Pelicantelope

This bird has a funny waddle,
But he's splendid when he flies.
His favorite dish is cold, raw fish,
And he has lovely eyes.

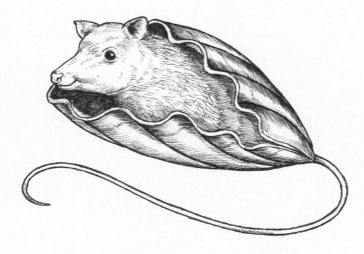

# The Scallopossum

This beast lives in the water
But is often found on land.
She loves to sit and sun herself
Upon the sad sea sand.

She's a most devoted parent,
And to please the little fry
She takes them from her pocket
And she hangs them out to dry.

# APPENDIX

*Being an alphabetic listing of other wondrous beasts encountered on my travels, accurately rendered and also depicted in the colored plates of this volume — for fellow zoologists possessing a sharp eye and a curious nature.*

| | | | |
|---|---|---|---|
| *Army Ant* | *Bullfinch* | *Bullfrog* | *Catbird* |
| *Catfish* | *Chocolate Moose* | *Clownfish* | *Cockatwo* |
| *Dandylion* | *Deer Mouse* | *Dragonfly* | *Fiddler Crab* |
| *Fly Ball* | *Fowl Ball* | *Fruit Bat* | *Horsefly* |